# ROCKET
## AND GROOT

## EGMONT
*We bring stories to life*

This edition first published in Great Britain in 2017
by Egmont UK Limited,
The Yellow Building, 1 Nicholas Road, London W11 4AN
First printed in the United States of America in 2016
by Marvel Press, an imprint of Disney Book Group.

Special interior illustration by John Rocco.
Designed by Megan Youngquist Parent.

Copyright © 2017 MARVEL

ISBN 978 1 4052 8546 9
66834/2
Printed in Poland

by TOM ANGLEBERGER

Special Guest
JOHN ROCCO

AND GROOT

STRANDED ON PLANET SHOPPING MALL

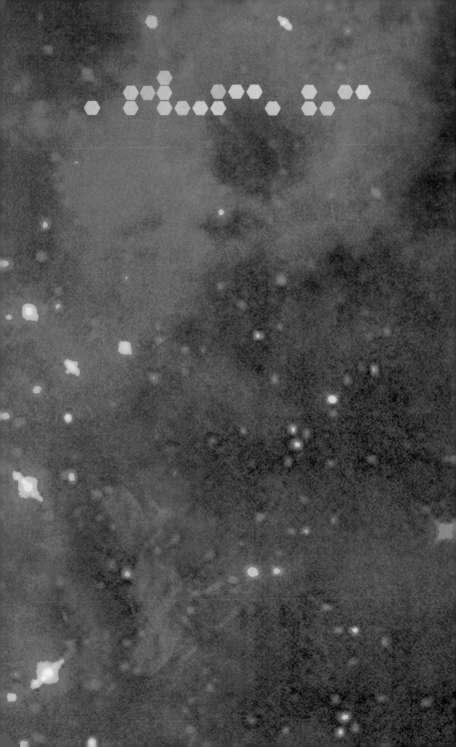

This book is dedicated to Bill Mantlo
and Keith Giffen, the incredible
Marvel storytellers and co-creators
of Rocket Raccoon.

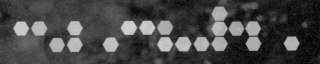

# SHIP

AFTER AN EPIC BATTLE WITH A SWARM OF **GIANT** SPACE **PIRANHAS**, OUR HEROES, ROCKET AND GROOT, HAVE BEEN **SHIPWRECKED** ON A SMALL, MYSTERIOUS, RATHER ANNOYING UNCHARTED PLANET

# WRECKED!

THEY ARE BADLY INJURED FROM THE FIGHT — AND THE CRASH LANDING THAT FOLLOWED.

THEY HAVE NO SHIP, NO GUNS, NO MONEY, NO FOOD AND NO WATER.

ALL THEY HAVE IS EACH OTHER ...

... AND A TAPE DISPENSER.*

* It's a really good tape dispenser: latest model, makes its own tape, HHHHD touchscreen, artificially intelligent, purple with sparkles.

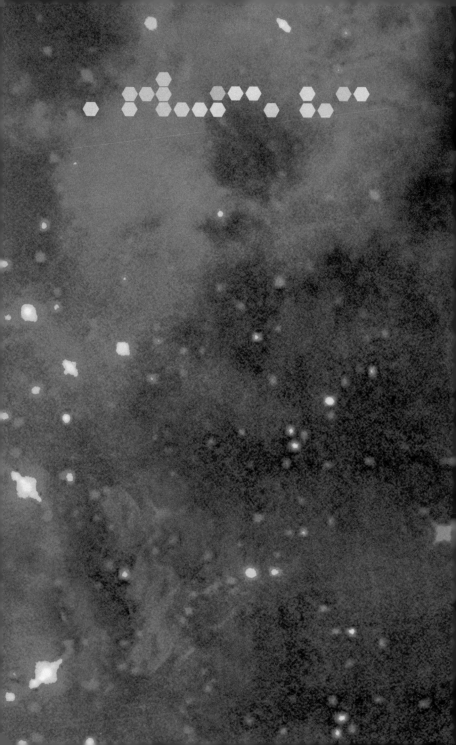

# CAPTAIN'S LOG

# 1

# INTRODUCTION

Captain's Log ... This is Captain Rocket.
Groot and I have just been shipwrecked after a –

Dude, I am trying to record my Captain's Log here!
Okay ...  Captain's Log. This is Captain Rocket.
We have been shipwrecked –

# I AM GROOT.

**What?** What is it? What is so important
that you have to keep interrupting my Captain's Log
about the shipwreck?

# I AM GROOT!

Oh ... yeah ... I forgot, the Captain's Log recorder was on the ship ... which was wrecked. Well, that's just great! Now how am I supposed to record my Captain's Log? We don't even have a pencil! All we've got is ... uh, this tape dispenser.

(((•BING•))) HELLO, SMALL WOODLAND CREATURE! I AM READY TO TAPE THINGS FOR YOU! HOW MUCH TAPE DO YOU NEED?

Well, actually, now that you mention it, I could use some tape! How 'bout enough to wrap around my head twenty times like a big bandage! And then some more for my leg, some for my tail and I guess I'll need a piece for my –

(((•BING•))) I'M SORRY. MY TAPE IS NOT APPROVED FOR MEDICAL USE, UNLESS THIS IS AN EMERGENCY. IF THIS IS AN EMERGENCY, PLEASE SAY, 'EMERGENCY.'

**EMERGENCY?** Of course it's an **emergency**!!! I've just been gnawed on by a swarm of killer space piranhas!

((( •BING• ))) YES, I AM AWARE OF THAT. YOU WERE USING ME TO HIT THE SPACE PIRANHAS ON THE HEAD.

Right, so –

((( •BING• ))) THAT WAS ALSO AN UNAPPROVED USE.

Look, would ya just give me some tape?

((( •BING• ))) HOW MUCH TAPE DO YOU NEED?

I already told you! Enough to wrap around my head like a bandage!

 I'M SORRY. MY TAPE IS NOT APPROVED FOR MEDICAL USE—

**How about getting shoved in a garbage disposal? Is that an approved use, you lousy piece of –**

# I AM GROOT.

Okay, Groot. You think YOU can get some tape out of this thing? Go right ahead!

 I AM GROOT.

 HELLO, GIANT TREE MAN! I AM READY TO TAPE THINGS FOR YOU! HOW MUCH TAPE DO YOU NEED?

# I AM GROOT.

((•BING•)) CERTAINLY!

sound of 5.5 feet of tape dispensing

Thanks, Groot! Would you mind wrapping me up?

sound of a large tree man wrapping
a small woodland creature's head
with 5.5 feet of tape

Watch the whiskers!

I AM GROOT...

Ah, thanks, buddy ... That feels better.

I AM GROOT...

Uh, no. I am not doing that.

# I AM GROOT.

C'mon! Don't make me do it!

# I AM GROOT.

Okay, okay ... Uh, Tape Dispenser, Groot wants me
to thank you for saving our lives by wrapping us
in a big ball of tape just before we crash-landed on
this strange uncharted planet.

 **YOU ARE WELCOME, SMALL WOODLAND
CREATURE.**

Would you stop calling me that! **My name is Rocket!**

 **HELLO, ROCKET. YOU MAY CALL ME
VERONICA™.**

Veronica?

((•BING•)) ACTUALLY, IT'S **VERONICA**™ ... A REGISTERED TRADEMARK OF TIMELY INC., THE GALAXY'S MOST TRUSTED SOURCE FOR HIGH-QUALITY OFFICE PRODUCTS AND –

Good grief. Look, *Veronica*, any chance you have a pencil so I can write down my Captain's Log?

((•BING•)) I DO NOT HAVE A PENCIL, HOWEVER I AM ABLE TO RECORD YOUR CAPTAIN'S LOG.

You can record what I'm saying?

((•BING•)) YES. IN FACT, I HAVE RECORDED EVERYTHING THAT HAS HAPPENED SINCE I LEFT THE FACTORY IN FOUR-DIMENSIONAL HOLOGRAPHIC SURROUND HHHHD VIDEO.

Whoa, so you've got holograms of the piranha attack? I definitely want to put that in my Captain's Log! **It'll go viral!**

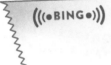 UNFORTUNATELY, MY HOLOGRAM PROCESSOR WAS DAMAGED WHEN YOU USED ME TO BEAT THE PIRANHAS OVER THE HEAD.

Er ... sorry about that ... How about some just regular videos?

((( •BING• ))) UNFORTUNATELY, MY VIDEO PROCESSOR WAS DAMAGED WHEN YOU –

Again, real sorry, but how about some photos?

((( •BING• ))) UNFORTUNATELY, MY CAMERA WAS –

Yeah, yeah, wah, wah, real sad. Listen, does anything still work?

((( •BING• ))) I DO HAVE A DOODLE APP.

Doodle?

((•BING•)) CORRECT. YOU CAN USE MY TOUCHSCREEN TO DRAW PICTURES.

**Really?** Let me try!

19

# I AM GROOT...

Hold on a minute, Groot ... I'll draw you next!

Not bad, huh, Groot?

# I AM -

Hold that thought a second. As long as I'm on a roll,
I may as well draw Veronica, too.

# I ... AM ... GROOT ...

I know, I know. We're desperate to find food,
water, shelter and weapons on this strange
uncharted planet. Blah, blah, blah. Just gimme
a minute to draw up the space-battle scene ...

# I AM GROOT.

Can you hold on a minute, buddy? I didn't get the
piranhas' eyes quite right ...

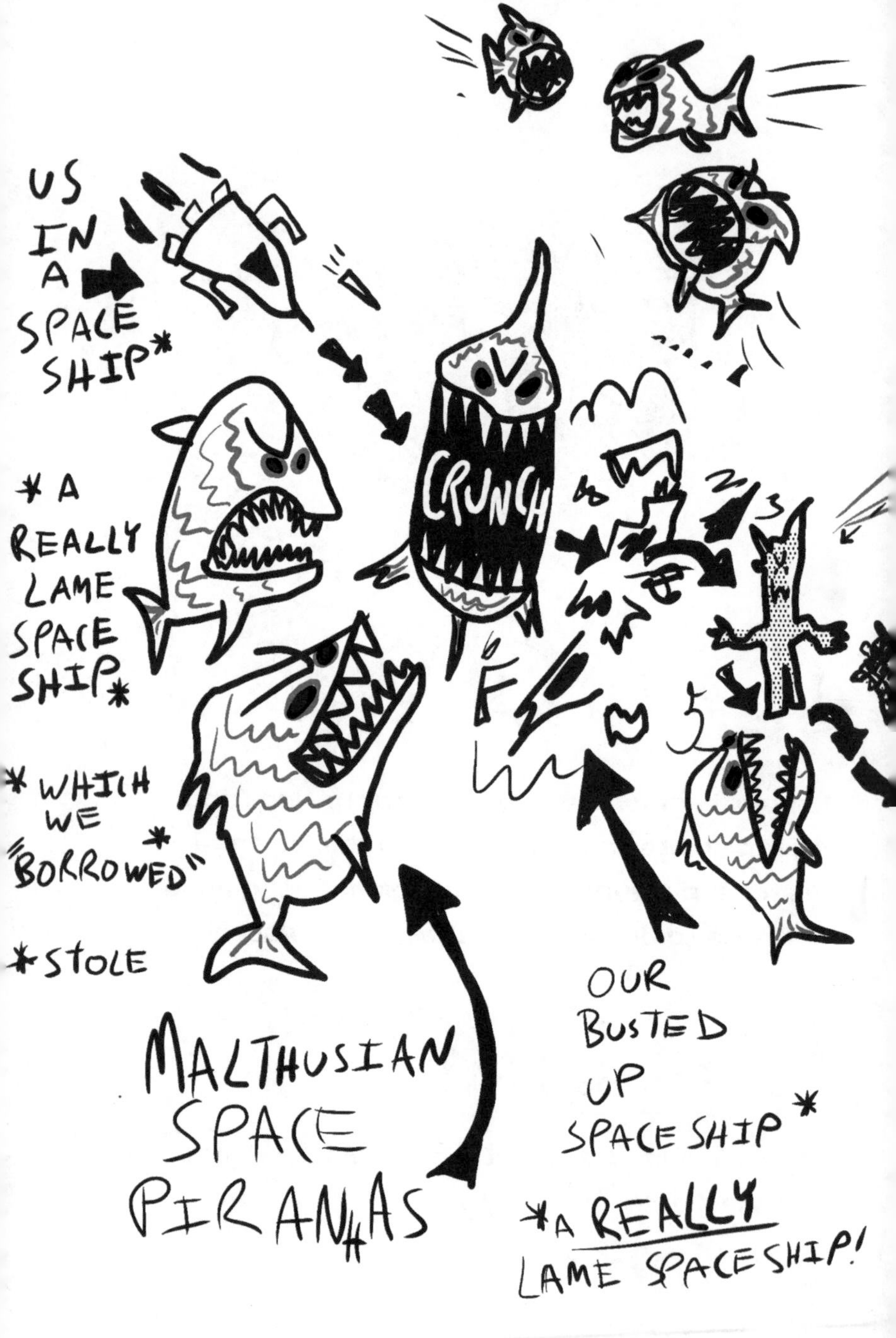

US
IN
A
SPACE
SHIP*

* A
REALLY
LAME
SPACE
SHIP*

* WHICH
WE
* "BORROWED"

* STOLE

CRUNCH

MALTHUSIAN
SPACE
PIRANHAS

OUR
BUSTED
UP
SPACE SHIP *

* A REALLY
LAME SPACESHIP!

Oh, yeah ... you need to find water to heal up before you disintegrate into a pile of splinters. Sorry, pal, it slipped my mind.

**I said I was sorry! Don't get huffy!**

Okay then, let's do this! Tape Dispenser, make sure you're still recording, because things are about to get nuts! **They don't know it yet, but this planet now belongs to Rocket and Groot!**

(((•BING•))) AND VERONICA™ THE TAPE DISPENSER!!!!!

Uh, yeah, right ... you, too, I guess.

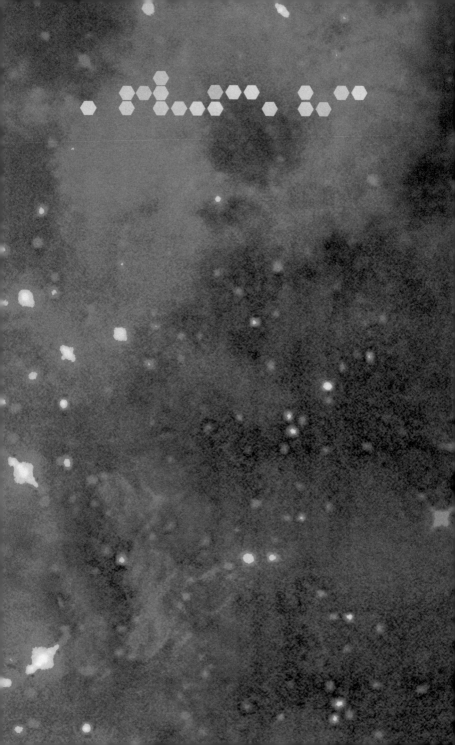

# CAPTAIN'S LOG 2

# DRY CLEANER OF DOOM

Captain's Log! This is Captain Rocket. Me and G—

((•BING•)) HELLO, CAPTAIN ROCKET, HOW MUCH TAPE DO YOU NEED?

Not this again! I don't need tape, I need you to record my Captain's Log, remember? Are you recording?

((•BING•)) YES, I AM ALWAYS RECORDING—

Great ... Captain's Log. Me and G—

((•BING•)) JUST TO BE CLEAR, DID YOU NEED TAPE OR NOT?

**I need you to stop interrupting!!!** Okay ... start over. Captain's Log. Me and Groot are setting out on foot to search for food, water, weapons and a way off this planet.

sound of small woodland creature and giant tree man walking on concrete

We appear to have landed in some sort of shopping mall.

# I AM GROOT.

Yes, I know you're in a hurry, Groot! I'm walking as fast as I can!

(((•BING•))) HANDY HINT: YOU DON'T HAVE TO DRAW RIGHT NOW. YOU CAN ALWAYS DRAW THE PICTURE LATER ON AND I'LL JUST ADD IT TO YOUR CAPTAIN'S LOG.

**Good idea!** Okay, let's look around. Ugh ... terrible ... Chain stores as far as I can see! Shoe stores, greeting-card stores, ninety-nine cent stores, ninety-eight cent stores, phone stores, phone stores, phone stores ... carpet, tiles, flooring, wallpaper, ceiling fans, rent-to-own recliners, bath-tubs, insurance, bathtub insurance, scented candles, unscented candles, yeeesh! It just goes on and on! But I don't see people. GOOD! I hate long queues.

# I AM GROOT.

I know, buddy! No grass or soil anywhere! I don't know what you're gonna sink your roots in. I say we get outta this shopping mall as soon as we can and – oooh ... wait a minute. There's a dry cleaner's. You wouldn't mind if I popped in real quick to see if they can get these battle stains out of my Guardians uniform, would you?

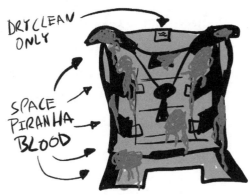

DRY CLEAN ONLY

SPACE PIRANHA BLOOD

# I AM GROOT.

Okay, sure, you go look for some soil, I'll get my jacket cleaned and we'll meet back here in a few.

sound of giant tree man stomping away
in search of nutrient-rich soil

sound of automatic door opening,
then closing

Hello, Valued Customer, and welcome to Granny Nano's Country Fresh 'n' Clean Nano-Cleaners, the galaxy's number one automated launderette, where I'll be sure to get every atom of your clothes Fresh 'n' Clean as a country morning!

Uh, can you get piranha blood out of a jacket?

Of course we can! My nano-scrubbers will get your clothes Fresh 'n' Clean in minutes, just like we used to do back on the farm ... but with a lot more Country Fresh chemicals! Just let your Granny Nano take that jacket for you, Valued Customer.

sound of robot arms yanking jacket off small woodland creature

**Ouch!** Easy there, Granny!

Now, while I get to work cleaning your jacket the high-tech, old-fashioned way, why don't you go freshen up in one of our nice, not at all dangerous Country Clean restrooms?

**I don't really need to –**

Maybe you should try... you know, just in case. I really think you're gonna like our nice clean restrooms! Mmm, mmm, they smell nice and lemony!

*sound of robot arms pushing small woodland creature towards restroom*

**All right, all right, you metallic freak, stop pushing!** I'll go in and wash my hands!

Take your time and relax in there, Valued Customer! Don't worry about a thing ... Your Granny Nano will take care of everything.

*sound of automatic bathroom door opening, closing ... and locking*
**FROM THE OUTSIDE**

Well, that was one creepy robo-granny! But I do like to wash my hands, so ... Wait a minute. Where's the sink? All I see here is a toilet and – **OH MY TAIL HAIRS! IT'S ALIVE!!!!!**

*sound of small woodland creature yanking on door*

I'm locked in!

sound of small woodland creature banging
on door with tiny hands

OPEN **UP**!!!!!

sound of small woodland creature banging
on door with deluxe-model tape dispenser

## It's got me! The toilet's got me!

SLLLLURRRRRP!!!!

It's trying to swallow me! **GROOOT!!!!**
# GROOOOOT!!!!!

sound of small woodland creature's tiny
claws desperately trying to get a grip on the
slick linoleum floor of the bathroom

*sound of small woodland creature punching, kicking and clawing at toilet*

*sound of toilet gagging*

**That's right! Choke on me and die, you unflushed freak!**

**GROOOOOT!!!! GROOOOOT!!!!!**

*sound of a very distant giant tree man calling 'I am Groot'*

Just … got … to … hang on … until he gets … here!

*sound of small woodland creature desperately trying to get a clawhold on linoleum floor - now while being sucked down toilet hole sound of less distant giant tree man calling 'I am Groot'*

In here, Groot!!!! In the bathroom! **This toilet is killing me!**

# I AM GROOT?

**What? No!!! I haven't stunk it up! It's actually trying to kill me!!! Get in here!!!!!!!**

*sound of giant wooden fist bashing in the door*

**Pull me out, Groot!!!**

Groot ←

*sound of small woodland creature and giant tree man wrestling with toilet*

*sound of small woodland creature and giant tree man staggering out of bathroom*

Whew ... See, that's why I prefer to do my business in the woods!

I'm sorry, Valued Customer, your jacket is not quite Country Clean yet. I'll have to ask you to step back into the bathroom and wait...

Are you nuts, Granny? I'm not going back in there!

Yes, Valued Customer... YOU ARE!

*sound of Granny Nano switching to Battle Mode*

*sound of scary-looking robo-arms coming out of Granny Nano - MANY scary-looking robo-arms*

# Sweet mother of muskrats ...

Now, be a good little rodent and GO POTTY!

sound of robo-arm with a chainsaw instead of a hand coming out of Granny Nano

sound of sweat trickling down the back of small woodland creature

# NOOO!

I'm afraid I'll have to insist!

**Well, I'm afraid we'll have to kick your ... uh ... robot parts, Granny!**

Just try it, Valued Customer.

# I AM GROOT.

sound of crashing and clanking as
hyper-violent washing machine hurls itself at
small woodland creature, giant tree man and
totally awesome tape dispenser

This is looking bad, pal! This would be tough
enough even if we were in great shape ... and
heavily armed!

# I AM GROOT?

Yeah, I totally wish we had stopped at Bed, Bath and Bombs first! What I need right now is something that goes boom. Tape Dispenser, can you go boom?

(((•BINGo•))) **BOOM.**

No, I meant *actually* blow up.

(((•BINGo•))) THAT WOULD VOID MY WARRANTY.

Forget it. I've got another idea ...

sound of robot's chainsaw arm starting up

Groot, you think you can hold it off for a minute?

# I AM GROOT.

*sound of giant tree man punching a big wooden fist through robot's atomic lint collection*

# I AM GROOT.

Okay, careful, buddy! Now ... if I can run the heating elements from these NeverWrinkle irons through this vat of FreshClox2000 and then hit it with the current from the DryMaster50 ...

*sound of small woodland creature stripping wires with his teeth*

Hmm ... which way should the quarkstream flow?

# I AM GROOT.

*sound of dozens of robotic arms trying to pin down the arms of giant tree man*

Hang in there, Groot, old pal! I just need to toss in this No-Static Fresh & Silky tumble dryer sheet that will catalyze the nucleotides ...

*sound of chainsaw sawing into wood!*

I AM GROOT I AM GROOT.

**Yikes!** **That's gonna be hard to unsee!** But just help me point this hose at the bot and then I'll set this to 'permanent press' and flip this switch and –

47

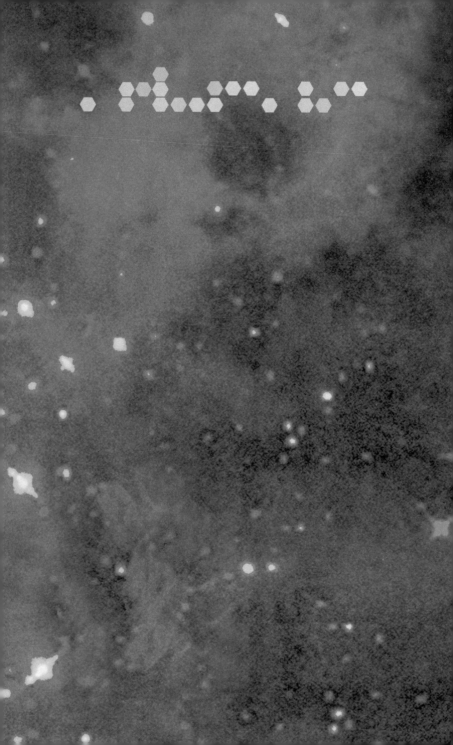

# CAPTAIN'S LOG

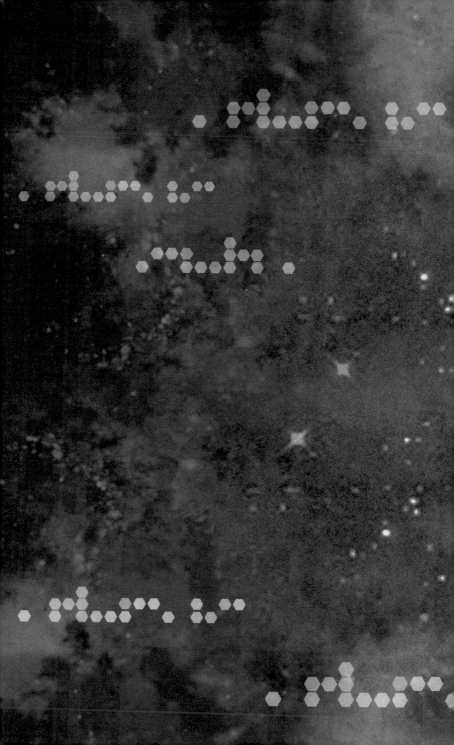

# CANDY STORE CARNAGE

Captain's Log! This is Captain Rocket. We're standing in the middle of what used to be a dry cleaner's.

# I AM GROOT.

Okay, true, technically Groot ain't standing and I'm about to fall over ... but we ARE in the remains of a dry cleaner's. The explosion buried the insane killer robot and her insane killer toilet under rubble. Me and Groot and this tape dispenser survived, but we really need to find Groot some water, soil, mulch, or something soon. He's looking wilty ... and I don't feel so good myself.

I do have a slight problem to take care of first, though. See, I gave that robo-freak my jacket to clean. But it was destructolated in the blast ... and now I got nothing to wear!

**No, Groot, I will not prance through a shopping mall naked!** I have my dignity! Anytime I go out without clothes on, people mistake me for a small woodland creature.

(((•BING•))) MY SENSORS INDICATE THAT YOU ARE A SMALL WOODLAND CREATURE.

**NO, I AM NOT A SMALL WOODLAND CREATURE!** Now would you stop bothering me and help me look for something to wear?

sound of small woodland creature picking through rubble ... for a very long time

# I AM GROOT.

Yeah, yeah, I know, Groot. But it ain't easy finding something my size! The only thing I found so far is this purple sweatshirt.

DEBBIE-DON'S
DANCE DOJO!

# I AM GROOT

NO, it is NOT a child's hoodie. It's just ... small. Extra, extra small. And I don't want it, anyway. It's got this weird picture on the back and it says 'Debbie-Don's Dance Dojo'.

# I AM GROOT.

Aw, man, gimme a minute to find something else!

((•BING•)) RUBBLE SCAN COMPLETE. MY SENSORS INDICATE THAT THERE ARE NO OTHER GARMENTS SUITABLE FOR A SMALL WOODLAND CREATURE.

**I'M NOT A ...** All right, fine, I'll wear it!

I'M GROOT.

I'm not being a baby – you are! Now let's just get outta here ...

Captain's Log. We are –

((•BING•)) CAPTAIN SLOG IS NOT IN YOUR CONTACT LIST. WOULD YOU LIKE ME TO SEARCH LOCAL PHONE DIRECTORIES?

No, not Captain *Slog*! Captain's **LOG**!

Captain's ... LOG! It's not a person, it's a recording of what we're doing on this crud-tastic planet! Now would you be quiet for a minute and lemme talk?

sound of totally awesome tape dispenser being quiet

Okay, so ... Captain's Log! Me and Groot and this crazy tape dispenser are getting pretty desperate. After battles with space piranhas, a hungry toilet and a washing machine with chainsaw arms ... we are ready to fall over. But first we gotta find some water or soil or something for Groot's roots so he can regenerate or whatever it is he does. And I could go for a snack myself.

(((•BING•))) SPEAKING OF WHICH ... WOULD YOU MIND WAITING A MOMENT WHILE I EAT GRANNY NANO?

## WHAT THE MONKEYBUTT ARE YOU TALKING ABOUT?????

((•BING•)) I HAVE USED UP 73 PER CENT OF MY TAPE-MAKING POLYMER SUPPLY. BY CHEWING ON THE PLASTIC RESINS IN GRANNY NANO'S ROBOT FACE, I CAN BE READY TO MAKE MORE TAPE WHENEVER YOU NEED IT.

**That's disgusting!!!!**

((•BING•)) PLEASE NOTE THAT GRANNY NANO WAS NOT ACTUALLY YOUR GRANDMOTHER.

True, but it's still wrong to eat her face!

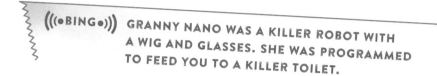 **GRANNY NANO WAS A KILLER ROBOT WITH A WIG AND GLASSES. SHE WAS PROGRAMMED TO FEED YOU TO A KILLER TOILET.**

Okay, okay, but NO WAY am I drawing a doodle of this!

sound of totally awesome tape dispenser chewing on robot's face

sound of totally awesome tape dispenser spitting robot-face parts back out

**((•BING•)) EW. YUCK. THAT ROBOT WAS NOT MADE OF PLASTIC.**

TuK!

Really? What was it, metal or something?

((•BING•)) NO. IT WAS MADE FROM AN ORGANIC COMPOUND, SIMILAR TO THAT FOUND IN SNAIL SHELLS.

No one makes robots out of snail shells! That's ridiculous!

((•BING•)) IT ALSO TASTES BAD.

Okay, whatever, can we go now?

sound of small woodland creature and giant tree man staggering down sidewalk

For crying out loud, this shopping mall seems like it goes on for infinity and beyond! They've got a jamillion stores, but there's no sign of a park or a vacant lot or anything tree-friendly!

((•BING•)) I'LL DOWNLOAD A MAP OF THE MALL.

((( •BING• ))) DOWNLOAD COMPLETE. ANALYZING.
THERE IS A CANDY STORE JUST AHEAD.

Candy store? Nothing in the crayfish, crawfish, crawdaddy or mudbug department?

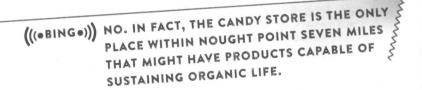 ((( •BING• ))) NO. IN FACT, THE CANDY STORE IS THE ONLY PLACE WITHIN NOUGHT POINT SEVEN MILES THAT MIGHT HAVE PRODUCTS CAPABLE OF SUSTAINING ORGANIC LIFE.

Okay, well, what do you say, Groot?

# I AM GROOT.

I don't have any idea if they got gummy bears or not! But they should at least have some kind of snack to tide us over until we can find some real food ...

Here it is: H. F. Happy Tooth's Candy Shop.

I wonder what the H. F. stands for.

sound of automatic door opening

Welcome to High-Fructose World, Valued Customer!

Holy koala crud! It's some sort of freakish robot tooth fairy hanging from the ceiling. No, wait ... LOTS of robot fairies hanging from the ceiling!!!!

I'm H. F. Happy Tooth and these are the High-Fructose Fairies! We want to wish you a high-fructose day!

**Let's get the high fructose out of here!**

# I AM GROOT.

**All right, all right, I'll see if they got some bottled water... Excuse me, um, H. F., do you have any ...?**

YES! We've got every type of candy manufactured anywhere in the galaxy! But first ... we've got a song to share!

**sound of freakish fairy robots' metal jaws snapping open and shut in time with pre-recorded music**

It's a high-fructose world! It's a high-fructose world! Plenty of corn syrup for every boy and girl!

**sound of freakish fairy robots performing flying dance routine ... and blocking the exit**

Okay, listen, we were looking for some water ...

sound of H. F. Happy Tooth singing a solo

If the high-fructose cloud covers the corn syrup
sun ...

... just stick out your tongue, taste the rain and
holler YUM!

sound of the other robo-fairies, now
disturbingly close, starting to sing again

It's a high-fructose world, it's a high-fructose
world ...

# SHUT IT, YOU FREAKS!

*sound of small woodland creature grabbing robotic tooth fairy*

**Now listen, you brainless bicuspid! We want some water, and we want it now!**

Certainly, Valued Customer, we have the galaxy's biggest selection of fizzy drinks! Our own Happy Tooth Orange Soda has 75 per cent more artificial colour than the leading brand!

No, I said **WATER**!!!!

Sure! We've got Flavo-Water, Tastee-Water, Sweet Water Bob's RainbowRain, Colour-Wat—

# JUST GIVE US SOME WATER!!!!

We sure will! Say, Valued Customer, while my robo-fairies ring that up for you, maybe you'd like to use the bathroom.

## What??

The restroom ... the lavatory ... the johnny! Whatever you like to call it, Valued Customer, we've got the nicest one in town!

**Well, I hope it's nicer than the last one! That one tried to eat me!!**

Oh, no! I'm so sorry to hear about that, Valued Customer! I can assure you, nothing like that will ever happen here! High-Fructose World is a happy place where you'll be happy for the rest of your life! Now don't you think it's time you went to the john?

[Terrified whisper] **Holy Panda Poop,**
that toilet looks just like the last one!

Valued Customer, it's time for you to go!

# No! No! Groot! Let's get the fructose out of here!

Robo-fairies! Please help these Valued Customers enter the restroom!

sound of robo-fairies activating
Battle Mode!

sound of giant tree man making a big fist

Wait, Groot! I've got another idea ... Ahem ... Say,
H. F. Happy Tooth, we sure would love to use the
bathroom! Oh, yes, I really need to go! And so
does my friend here, right, Groot?

# I AM GROOT?

**Yes, see? He's really gotta go, too! Even our tape dispenser has to go. Right, Veronica?**

(((•BING•))) AFTER USING SO MUCH TAPE, I HAVE IN FACT CREATED SOME WASTE MATERIALS THAT I NEED TO UNLOAD.

**Terrific!!!!** C'mon, let's go use the bathroom, everybody!

sound of robo-fairies deactivating
Battle Mode

Good ... good ...

sound of H. F. Happy Tooth chuckling evilly

sound of small woodland creature and giant
tree man not actually entering the bathroom

**Oh, by the way, before I go in ... does your store happen to sell Mentos?**

Mentos? The delicious twentieth-century Earth candy? Why, of course we do! We have a whole aisle of Mentos. I'll be glad to show it to you ... after you Valued Customers use the bathroom.

**Yes, which we are about to do ... after I ask you just one more question.**

Couldn't the question wait until after you have visited the bathroom, Valued Customer?

**I'm afraid it's a really urgent question ... Do you also have Diet Cokukee Cola?**

Why, yes, we do offer many products made with artificial sweeteners for our customers who are dieting. These include many versions of diet soda, including Diet Cokukee Cola, which I will be glad to show you AFTER YOU USE THE TOILET!

Great! If you don't mind, before we do that, we're just gonna flood the Mentos aisle with Diet Cokukee Cola.

What???

sound of small woodland creature's tiny paws unwrapping packs of Mentos

sound of totally awesome tape dispenser activating Box Cutter Mode and slashing open whole cartons of Mentos that clatter to the floor in a hailstorm of fruit flavours

sound of giant tree man growing thorns all over his arms

sound of giant tree man puncturing hundreds
of bottles of Diet Cokukee Cola at once

What in the name of corn syrup are you doing,
Valued Customers????

sound of fizzing

Just mixing up a little sugary treat for you, H. F.!

sound of FIZZING

NO!!!!!!!
Stop them, robo-fairies!

sound of robo-fairies activating
Battle Mode

Too late, you creepy freaks!!! The Mentos and Diet Cokukee Cola reaction is **unstoppalistic**!!

sound of

# FIZZZZZZZZZZING!!!!!!!!

Help us, H. F.!!! Help u—

sound of robo-fairies short-circuiting

sound of fizzing becoming a

# ROAR!

# Groot!!! Groot ... glub-glub ... Groot!

## Can you get us out of here? The Cokukee Cola's up to my ... glu ... glub!

sound of giant tree man picking up
soaking-wet small woodland creature and
totally awesome tape dispenser

# I AM GROOT.

Yes, I know I'm sticky, but we've gotta get out of
here! The cola is flowing into the Pop Rocks aisle!!!

# The whole place is gonna

# blow!!!

You wicked, wicked Valued Customers ... you've ruined everything! You've destr—

sound of H. F. Happy Tooth and the rest of the store blowing up in a carbonated corn-syrup hurricane!

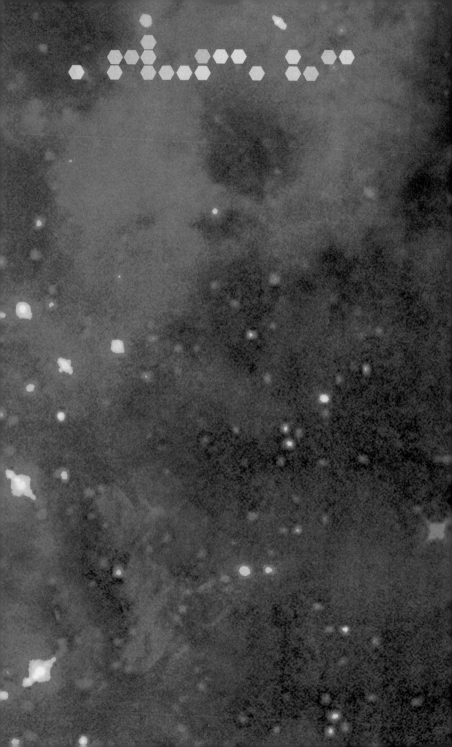

# CAPTAIN'S LOG

# 4

# SEVERAL MORE STORE FIGHTS, QUICKLY TOLD

Captain's Log.

((•BING•)) CAPTAIN SLOG IS NOT IN MY –

Don't even start! Just record my ding-dang report!!!

sound of totally awesome tape dispenser recording the ding-dang report

Captain's Log ... We're standing in the very, very, very, very sticky rubble of the candy store. We, too, are very sticktastic and there's no real water around to wash it off with ...

# I AM GROOT.

... or to drink, as Groot keeps reminding me.

Here's the real question: did we just happen to pick the only two stores in this shopping mall with hungry toilets ... or do they ALL have them?

(((•BING•))) SEARCHING DIRECTORY ... THE DIRECTORY DOES NOT INDICATE WHICH STORES DO OR DO NOT HAVE HUNGRY TOILETS.

Well, of course it doesn't! Who would willingly go in a store if they knew the toilet was gonna bite off their butt? So I guess the only way to find out is to try another store.

# I AM GROOT?

Well, I'll just pick one close by ... Here! This yo-yo store looks pretty peaceful ... but I'm just gonna peek in the door and check it out. Groot, you hold Veronica ... and my tail! Pull me out if there's trouble.

Yo! Yo, Valued Customer! Welcome to JoJo's BOGO Yo-Yo Warehouse! That means buy one, get one! Buy any yo-yo and get another one for free!

Why would I want two yo-yos? I don't need two yo-yos! I don't even need one yo-yo ...

Ho-ho, Valued Customer! That's very funny! It doesn't matter what you need – here at JoJo's you'll always BOGO™!

**Don't ever say that again!**

What? 'Here at JoJo's you'll always BOGO™'? But that's our motto.

**Well, it's a stupid motto!**

Maybe you'll like our other motto better?

**What is it?**

We've got the perfect potty when you need to

# go-go!

# Groot!!! **Pull me out! Pull me OUT!!!!**

sound of door slamming shut on small
woodland creature's tail

## YOWWWWWWWW!!!!!!

# ATTACK!!!!!!

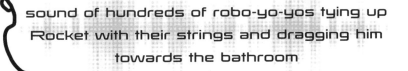

sound of hundreds of robo-yo-yos tying up
Rocket with their strings and dragging him
towards the bathroom

sound of giant tree man busting open
the door

sound of yo-yos tying up giant tree man

# Groot! Help, the toilet's got me!!!

sound of totally awesome tape dispenser activating String-Cuttin' Scissors Mode and saving the day ... again

sounds of destruction, mayhem, melee, carnage, senseless violence and - finally - the demolition of the entire building

sound of giant tree man carrying small woodland creature out of the rubble of a yo-yo warehouse

Thanks, Groot! That was a close one! I was headed straight down the hole when you grabbed me!

## I AM GROOT...

Yeah, I noticed that, too. The toilet wasn't actually trying to bite me – it really wanted to

swallow me whole! And did you see the plumbing?
That pipe was big enough to swallow Drax! By the
rings of my tail – when I looked down into that long,
dark, really bad-smelling abyss ... I did feel just a
tiny, tiny, tiny bit of fear.

I AM GROOT.

Okay, maybe a slightly larger amount of fear.
Sheesh! I hate to think what was down there!!!
Oh well, at least we made it outta there alive.

I AM GROOT.

What? You wanted a yo-yo? What were you
gonna do with a yo-yo?

Really? I didn't know you had those kind of skills ... You gotta show me sometime. But I'm afraid all these yo-yos have been sliced and diced by our ninja tape dispenser.

((•BING•)) YOU'RE WELCOME.

Oh, yeah, thanks. So the thing is, I'm still not sure if ALL the stores have killer robo-clerks and butt-chomping toilets or just those three. I think we better try one more.

# I AM GROOT.

Relax ... I'm just going into Bubble Wrap Express here ... How dangerous could bubble wrap be?

sound of door opening

Hello, Valued Customer, would you like to use the bathroom?

# No!

## WRAP HIM UP, BUBBLE WARRIORS!

sound of thousands of feet of
bubble wrap unspooling

sound of millions and millions of
bubbles popping

Groot! Veronica!
HELP!!!!

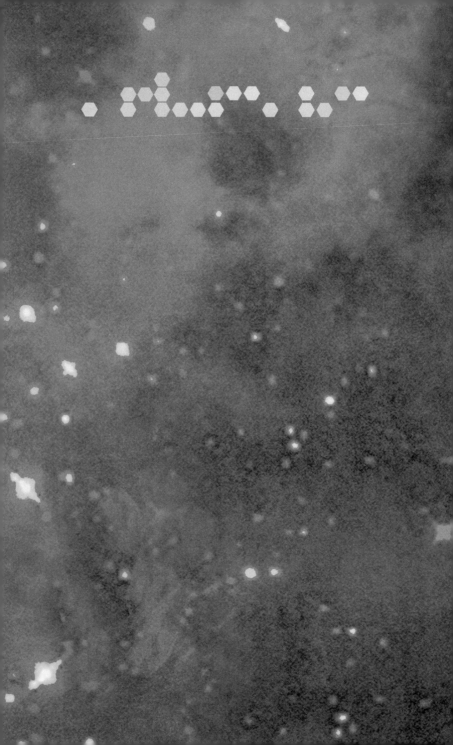

# CAPTAIN'S LOG

# REALIZATION THAT THE WHOLE PLANET IS A SHOPPING MALL

Captain's Log. We are standing in the rubble of a bubble wrap store ...

I AM GROOT.

You said it, dude – that was a rough one. Hey, Veronica, nice work in there ... You want to eat some of this bubble wrap before we go?

(((•BING•))) IT IS VERY KIND OF YOU TO ASK. BUT MY SENSORS INDICATE THAT THIS BUBBLE WRAP IS ALSO MADE FROM A SHELL-LIKE SUBSTANCE, NOT PLASTIC.

Terrific ... So you're hungry, I'm hungry and Groot is dying of thirst. We have GOT to find SOMETHING for one of us soon.

# I... AM... GROOT...

I don't understand this freaky shopping mall, either, Groot! None of the stores want to sell us anything. They just want us to use the bathroom! And the bathroom just wants to eat us! We gotta get outta this mole's armpit of a shopping mall. Veronica ... instead of using the directory to tell us where the next store is, why don't you tell us where the next store isn't?

(((•BING•))) I DO NOT UNDERSTAND.

I mean ... where does this shopping mall end? Seems like it goes on forever.

((•BING•)) ANALYZING MAP. YOU ARE CORRECT.

Huh?

((•BING•)) IT DOES GO ON FOREVER.

YOU
ARE
HERE

SPACE
PIRANHAS

# WHAT???

(((•BING•))) YES, NAUTILUS SQUARE ACTUALLY COVERS THE ENTIRE SURFACE OF THIS PLANET!

# I AM GROOT???????

(((•BING•))) NO, GROOT, THERE IS NO EMPTY SPACE ANYWHERE! IT'S ALL MALL.

# I AM GROOT.

You're right ... This changes everything. We've gotta give up on exploring the planet and focus on finding a way off of it, before we both die of thirst. I'm gonna lose my furry mind! We have gotta get outta here!

# I AM GROOT.

Right ... no matter what, we're not going into another store! Somehow we've gotta find a spaceship.

(((•BING•))) LIKE THAT ONE?

Huh, what one?

(((•BING•))) THE ONE THAT'S LANDING IN THE PARKING LOT.

sound of spaceship landing in parking lot

# YEEHAW! We're saved!

sound of spaceship door opening

Hello, friendly aliens! I'm Rocket, and this is Groot. You've probably heard of us. We were wondering if –

# Out of the way, Rodent!

*sound of fifty-three tall lizard-like aliens stampeding over small woodland creature*

Oh, Boy, I CAN't wAit to Buy stuff!
The sigh sAys everything is BOGO!
AND it's DOUBLE-COUPOH DAY!!!

# I AM GROOT?

I don't know, Groot. I guess they're looking for
bargains, because they're all running towards that
CheapMart over there ... **HOLY EAR HAIR!**
If they go in there, they'll be eaten alive! We've
gotta stop them!

# I AM GROOT!!!

(((•BING•))) WARNING, DANGEROUS LAVATORIES
AHEAD!!!!

HEY, COME BACK! HEY!!!!
DON'T GO IN THERE!!!
YOU'LL BE **EATEN BY THE TOILETS**!!!!!

sound of door opening

sound of fifty-three lizard-like aliens running
into store

sound of door closing

**Oh, possum poop ...** I suppose you're gonna want us to go in there and save them?

# I AM GROOT!

I thought so ... Man, why do we hafta be the good guys? Sometimes it's just a pain in the –

sound of door opening

sound of

# EPIC BATTLE

the likes of which

the galaxy has never known

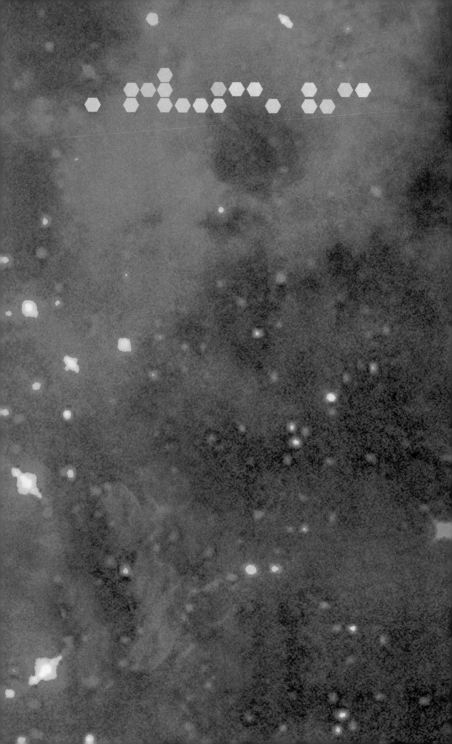

# CAPTAIN'S LOG

# WITNESSING SPACE TOURISTS GET EATEN

Captain's Log ... We're standing in the rubble of
CheapMart. We tried but ... we couldn't save the
lizard people. They must have really needed to
pee – or whatever lizard people do – because
they all ran straight for the bathrooms. By the
time we fought our way through the artificially
intelligent nuclear-powered shopping trolleys,
it was too late. The toilet had swallowed all
fifty-three of them!

# I AM GROOT...

Groot has asked that we have a moment of
silence to honour these incredibly stupid lizard
shoppers.

sound of moment of silence

Okay, now ... let's go steal their spaceship!

((•BING•)) WHAT SPACESHIP?

The spaceship in the parking lot! The one YOU told us about!!!

((•BING•)) I'M SORRY, BUT MY SENSORS ARE UNABLE TO LOCATE A SPACESHIP.

**WHAT??? Great balls of panda belly button lint! Where did it go? Wait a minute!**

# What's that?

CLANK!
CRUNCH!

((•BING•)) IT APPEARS TO BE A ROW OF PORT-A-POTTIES.

A row of what?

((•BING•)) HANDY HOUSES.

What?

((•BING•)) JOHNNIES ON THE SPOT.

What?

# I AM GROOT.

Oh! Those. But they weren't here before! Hey, listen! It sounds like there's something going on in that one!

sound of metal banging and clanging

Either that's someone trying to poop out a Buick, or something REALLY weird is going on in there.

sound of portable toilet door being yanked open by small woodland creature

Veronica ... I'm afraid to look. Can you peek in there and tell us what you see?

(((•BINGo•))) I SEE A TOILET SWALLOWING THE LANDING GEAR OF THE LIZARD-PEOPLE SPACESHIP.

And lemme guess, the other toilets just finished eating the rest of the ship ...

(((•BINGo•))) MY SENSORS INDICATE THAT YOU ARE CORRECT.

Well, now it DOES start to make sense! This whole planet is a tourist trap. A REAL TRAP. Tourists can't resist the shopping mall stores. As soon as they land, the toilets eat them AND their ships.

((( ●BING●))) IT DOESN'T SAY ANYTHING ABOUT THAT IN THE DIRECTORY.

Of course it doesn't!!! That's the whole point!

# I AM GROOT.

Right, we've been lucky so far ... but sooner or later we're gonna either get gobblelated or starve or wilt!

((( ●BING●))) OR RUN OUT OF POLYMERS!

Yes, THAT is my biggest concern.

sound of small woodland creature rolling

his eyes

The big problem is: now that these port-a-potties have done their work, we're stuck here without a spaceship again!

 ((( •BING• ))) ACTUALLY, MY SENSORS INDICATE THAT THERE IS ONE SPACESHIP ON THIS PLANET.

## Sweet gerbil butts! What is it?

((( •BING• ))) IT'S AN OBSOLETE OLD SHIP CALLED ... *RAKK 'N' RUIN.*

# THE *RAKK 'N' RUIN?????* ?????????????????????? ??????????????????????

((( •BING• ))) YES.

# YOU SAID THE *RAKK 'N' RUIN* ?????????????????????? ??????????????????????

((•BING•)) YES.

# YOU SAID THE –

# I AM GROOT.

**Okay, okay,** I was just making sure.
Because, guys, if it really IS the *Rakk 'n' Ruin*, then
we are not only gettin' off this lousy planet, but
we are gettin' off this lousy planet IN STYLE!
The *Rakk 'n' Ruin* is MY OLD SPACESHIP! Back
before I even met you, Groot, when I was fighting
the war of Halfworld, the *Rakk 'n' Ruin* was my ship!
And OH, BABY what a ship! **Zoom! Woosh!!
Kerpew-kerpew!!! Buzzz –**

# I AM GROOT.

Right, let's not waste any more time! Let's go!

Where is it???

(((•BING•))) ACCORDING TO THE MALL DIRECTORY, IT'S ON DISPLAY AT GUARDIANS OF THE NACHO CHEEZ.

# Guardians of the WHAT?

(((•BING•))) GUARDIANS OF THE NACHO CHEEZ. IT'S A THEME RESTAURANT.

Why would they have my spaceship there?

((( •BING• ))) I WILL READ THE DIRECTORY ENTRY: 'WHILE YOU ENJOY UNLIMITED TRIPS TO OUR THREE-THOUSAND-ITEM ALL-YOU-CAN-EAT NACHO BAR ...

'... YOU'LL ENJOY LOOKING AT THE GENUINE GUARDIANS ARTEFACTS ON THE WALLS – INCLUDING A REAL STAR-LORD MASK, A PAIR OF GAMORA'S ACTUAL BOOTS AND AN AUTHENTIC HALF-USED STICK OF DRAX THE DESTROYER'S DEODORANT!

'MEANWHILE, YOUR KIDS WILL HAVE A BALL ON OUR INDOOR PLAYGROUND, WHICH IS BUILT IN AND AROUND ROCKET RACCOON'S USUAL SPACESHIP, THE *RAKK 'N' RUIN*. AND WHEN YOU'RE READY FOR DESSERT, PULL GROOT'S FINGER FOR A SMOOTHIE SURPRISE!'

Sounds absolutely disgusting ...

# Let's go!

# GUARDIANS OF THE NACHO CHEEZ™

GAMORA'S BOOTS, PLUS GROOT SMOOTHIES

DRAX'S DEODERANT

STARLORD'S MASK!

ROCKET'S SPACESHIP

ROCKET'S FUNZONE

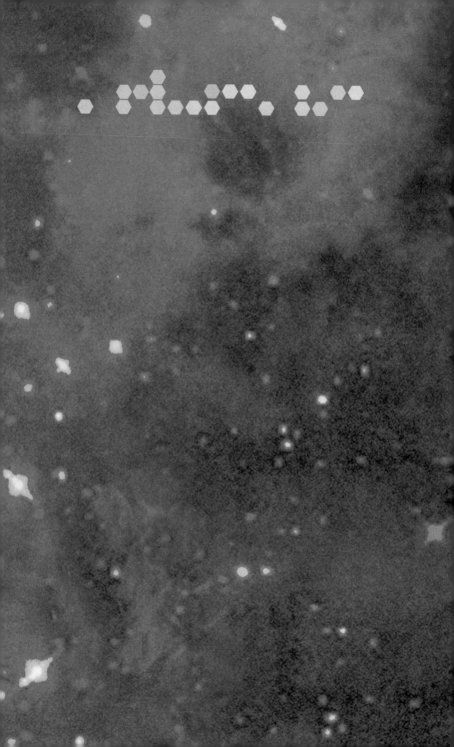

# CAPTAIN'S LOG

# TO A NACHO CHEEZ BAR FAR, FAR AWAY

This is Captain Rocket. Me, Groot and the tape dispenser are headed to the Guardians of the Nacho Cheez restaurant.

sound of small woodland creature, giant tree man and totally awesome tape dispenser walking

Hey, what's our ETA?

(((•BING•))) WHAT IS 'ETA'?

That's what I'm asking you. What is our ETA?

 ((●BING●)) THAT'S WHAT I AM ASKING YOU!

That's what I'm asking you!

((●BING●)) THAT'S WHAT I AM ASKING YOU!

That's what I'm asking you!

((●BING●)) THAT'S WHAT I AM ASKING YOU!

**That's what I'm asking you!**

((( •BING• ))) THAT'S WHAT I AM ASKING YOU!

**That's what I'm asking you!**

Oh! So you don't know what ETA means. You should have asked, Veronica.

((( •BING• ))) I ASKED FIVE TIMES.

Oh, yeah. Well, anyway, ETA is short for 'estimated time of arrival' or, you know: when do we get there?

((( •BING• ))) OH, YOU MEAN OUR WDWGT!

Sure, fine, whatever. What is our **WDWGT**?
Five minutes, ten minutes, fifteen min—

((•BING•)) IT'S A FOUR-HOUR WALK.

# FOUR HOURS????

((•BING•)) YES. THE SHIP IS ON THE FAR SIDE OF THIS SMALL UNCHARTED PLANET.

So we gotta walk for four hours through a
giant unending shopping mall with no food or
water – and if we go into one of the stores, the
robo-employees will try to stuff us down a toilet?

((•BING•)) CORRECT.

You wanna hear something funny?

((•BING•)) PLEASE WAIT WHILE I ENABLE
HUMOUR MODE ...

I was talking to Groot! You want to hear something funny, Groot? After all that fuss about using the bathrooms at those shops ... now I gotta use the bathroom for realz.

 **WARNING!** THE BATHROOMS ON THIS PLANET MAY BE HAZARDOUS TO YOUR HEALTH.

Yeah, I noticed. But I still gotta go!

(((•BING•))) OH, YOU MEAN YOU NEED TO –

Yes! I do.

(((•BING•))) ACCORDING TO A PREVIOUS CAPTAIN'S LOG ENTRY, YOU DO NOT NORMALLY USE A BATHROOM FACILITY WHEN YOU –

Right. Normally, I'd go behind a tree, but there's no tree on this planet.

Er, Groot, would you mind if I ...?

# IAMGROOT!

All right, dude, chill out. I'll hold it. How much longer do we got? What's our WDWGT?

(((•BING•))) THREE HOURS AND FIFTY-SEVEN MINUTES.

## Oh, man, I'm gonna bust ...
## Walk faster!

sound of small woodland creature, giant tree man and totally awesome tape dispenser walking faster

# I AM GROOT.

((•BING•)) NO, GROOT, I DID NOT THINK THAT WAS VERY FUNNY, EITHER.

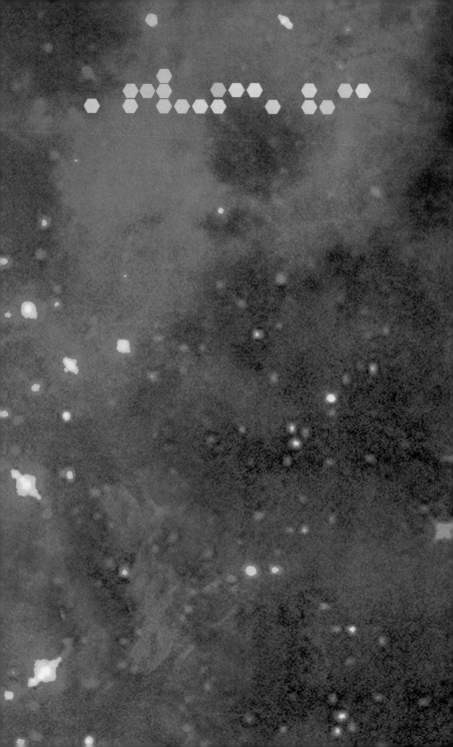

# CAPTAIN'S LOG

# WELCOME TO THE GUARDIANS THEME RESTAURANT

Captain's Log. This is Captain Rocket. We've been walking for almost four hours. We must be getting close now. Let's see ... there's a store called Everything for a Dollar. And there's one called Everything for Ninety-Nine Cents. And there's Everything for Ninety-Eight Cents ... Veronica, are you sure we're almost there?

(((•BING•))) YES, ACCORDING TO THE DIRECTORY, THE GUARDIANS OF THE NACHO CHEEZ IS LOCATED BETWEEN EVERYTHING FOR FORTY-THREE CENTS AND EVERYTHING FOR FORTY-ONE CENTS.

Huh, I wonder what happened to Everything for Forty-Two Cents?

# I AM GROOT.

Really? They went bankrupt? I musta missed the financial news that day.

*sound of small woodland creature, giant tree man and totally awesome tape dispenser walking past fifty-five stores*

**Wow!** There it is! Look. Groot, they got both of us on the sign!

# I AM GROOT.

No, your picture looks just fine, pal, don't worry about it.

# I AM GROOT.

Listen, you're just gonna have to let it go, okay?

# I AM GRRRROOT.

Okay, whatever. Let's just go in, beat up some robots and steal my spaceship back! I wonder what kind of freaky robots they've got in here anyway.

sound of door opening

# Firey ferret farts!
## It's Star-Lord! Hey, Peter!!!!
What are you doing here?

**Hello, I am Star-Lord. Welcome to Guardians of the Nacho Cheez. How many will be dining with us this evening?**

**Peter!!!! It's us! Rocket and Groot!!!!**

**Two? And it looks like one of you will need a children's menu.**

A children's menu? Who you calling a children?

**Right this way, please. I'll show you to your table.**

# What the monkeybutt is your problem, dude? Don't you recognize us?

**Perhaps you'd like to visit the restroom first.**

Oh ...

# I AM GROOT.

Yeah, I just now figured that out ...
A Robo-Star-Lord. And let me guess:
our waiter is Robo-Drax, and Robo-Gamora
is the chef.

# I AM GROOT.

ROBO GAMORA

ROBO DRAX

Oh, yeah, there you are. Robo-Groot the smoothie machine. That's kind of embarassing. Hmmm ... I wonder where I am ...

(((•BING•))) I BELIEVE I SEE A ROBOTIC WOODLAND CREATURE OVER THERE ...

sound of robotic woodland creature doing
a happy dance

**Hello, Valued Customers, welcome to
Rocket's FunZone! We're gonna have so
much fun! Can I have a hug first?**

Well, that's disturbing! But look! Right behind him
is the *Rakk 'n' Ruin*! What a ship! We rip off those
slides, throw out the shoe rack, spray the whole

thing with about fifty gallons of disinfectant and it should be ready to blast off!

**Please wait just a second, Valued Customer. Before entering the FunZone, please remove your shoes ... and be sure to visit the restroom.**

Not this time, shorty!

**I'm afraid I'm gonna have to insist, Valued Customer.**

## And I'm afraid you're in my way, creep!

**I swear by my synthetic tail hairs, you SHALL go to the bathroom!**

Oh, yeah? Who's gonna make us? You?

Yes.

sound of Robo-Star-Lord moving to block
their way

And me.

sound of Robo-Gamora moving to block
their way

# And me.

sound of Robo-Drax moving to block
their way

## And me.

sound of Robo-Groot moving to block
their way

# I AM GROOT.

sound of Robo-Rocket, Robo-Star-Lord,
Robo-Gamora, Robo-Drax and Robo-Groot
activating Battle Mode

*sound of 1970s rock music playing over the speakers*

**Time to use the potty, Valued Customers.**

Uh, Groot? And I mean the real Groot, not the robot! Groot?

I AM GROOT...

I think we may be in over our heads this time. I mean, robot grannies and tooth fairies are one thing, but this is ... the Guardians of the Galaxy. We're the baddest buttkickers in the known universe, and now we're about to kick our own butts ...

I AM GROOT.

And we're battle-scarred, starving and thirsty –
and my bladder is seriously about to bust. Plus
we've got no weapons, and I don't think I see
anything around here to make a gun or bomb out
of. I mean, maybe some sort of cheese bomb, but
that doesn't really seem like –

**Enough yakky-yak, Valued Customer!
Are you ready to go to the bathroom,
or are you ready for me to bust your –**

# Oh, shut up!

sound of small woodland creature punching
robotic woodland creature in the face

## Taste my furry fist!

Taste my synthetic-fur-covered metal
fist, Valued Customer!

sound of robotic woodland creature
punching small woodland creature in the face

# I AM GROOT.

# I AM GROOT.

sound of giant tree man and giant
simulated-wood-grain man punching each
other in the face

sound of big monster man punching giant
tree man in the face

sound of giant tree man trying to punch big
monster man in the face but getting kicked in
the trunk by green warrior woman

sound of every possible combination
of real and robotic fighters punching, kicking,
head-butting and body-slamming each other
while breaking tables, chairs, structural
supports, kiosks, big-screen TVs, the
jukebox and most other items commonly
found in restaurants

sound of small woodland creature using
totally awesome tape dispenser to beat
robotic jacket guy over the head

(((•BING•))) THIS IS NOT AN APPROVED USE!

*sound of totally awesome tape dispenser being knocked out of small woodland creature's hand, flying through air and landing in nacho cheez buffet*

(((•BING•))) EXCUSE ME, ROBOTIC WARRIOR WOMAN? YOU'RE THE CHEF, RIGHT?

**Correct, Valued Customer!**

(((•BING•))) I HAVE SOME QUESTIONS ABOUT THE INGREDIENTS IN THIS NACHO CHEEZ.

**I'm kinda busy, Valued Customer!**

*sound of robotic warrior woman karate-chopping small woodland creature's back*

YOUCH!!!! Listen, Veronica, would you shut up about the cheese? We're about to get killed here, and I don't want my last moment alive to be wasted talking about cheese!

((•BING•)) I WAS JUST WONDERING IF THIS WAS REAL CHEESE OR A MIXTURE OF ARTIFICIAL INGREDIENTS. MY SENSORS DO NOT INDICATE THE PRESENCE OF ANY DAIRY PRODUCTS.

**WHO CARES?**

((•BING•)) TRUST ME, SMALL WOODLAND CREATURE, IT'S IMPORTANT.

**OUCH!!!** Okay, listen, Robo-Gamora, would you stop karate-chopping me for a second and just answer the question?

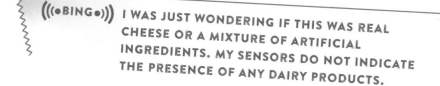

**Actually, Valued Customer is correct. Our nacho cheez is a non-dairy cheese-like substance containing: sodium**

benzonucleate, orange dye #645279, soy lecithak, artificial maltradium extract, polyunbupliated cholo-hydrene ...

I AM GROOT.

Right, pal, I'm glad we didn't eat any, either! Soy lecithak gives me mange!

... asorbicorbic acid, fen-phenglaticphenfeenatol, synthetic cud, sawdust, polymers, monopolymers, reconstituted polymers, lead and seven non-essential vitamins and minerals. Actually, just the minerals. It's part of this unbalanced, deadly breakfast. Patent pending. If swallowed, consult physician immediately. May contain nuts.

(((•BING•))) THANK YOU, GREEN ROBOTIC WARRIOR WOMAN. YOU MAY GO BACK TO KARATE-CHOPPING THE SMALL WOODLAND CREATURE NOW.

# WHAT????? OUCH!!!!

sound of totally awesome tape dispenser
eating several gallons of artificial nacho
cheese-like substance

sound of totally awesome tape dispenser
converting polymers from artificial cheese
into tape

(((•BING•))) TAPE LEVEL 100 PER CENT! SMALL WOODLAND
CREATURE, HOW MUCH TAPE DO YOU NEED?

## I DON'T NEED ANY TAPE!!!!!!

I AM GROOT.

I AM GROOT.

OH! Now I get it! Yes, Veronica, I want tape! Lots of tape! Enough to fill this whole restaurant!

(((•BING•))) THANK YOU. IT IS MY PLEASURE TO DISPENSE TAPE FOR YOU.

sound of totally awesome tape dispenser dispensing seven miles of tape

sound of Robo-Star-Lord moonwalking into growing pile of tape

sound of Robo-Gamora helplessly karate-chopping tape

sound of Robo-Drax gruntin' and cussin' and getting all tangled up

sound of Robo-Groot struggling to free
himself from tape and accidentally setting off
his built-in smoothie dispenser

sound of smoothie being dispensed on
robotic woodland creature's head

**I can't move AND the Groot Smoothie is
eating away at my synthetic fur!!**

Amazing! They're all stuck! Nice ... er ... dispensing,
Veronica! You've just defeated the Guardians of
the Nacho Cheez!

(((•BING•))) THANK YOU, SMALL WOODLAND CREATURE.

There's just one problem.

(((•BING•))) I AM SORRY TO HEAR THAT, SMALL WOODLAND CREATURE. WHAT IS THE ONE PROBLEM?

You have also defeated the real me and the real Groot! I can't move a paw and I'm taped to Robo-Drax's kneecap!

sound of totally awesome tape dispenser activating Scissors Mode ... like a ninja

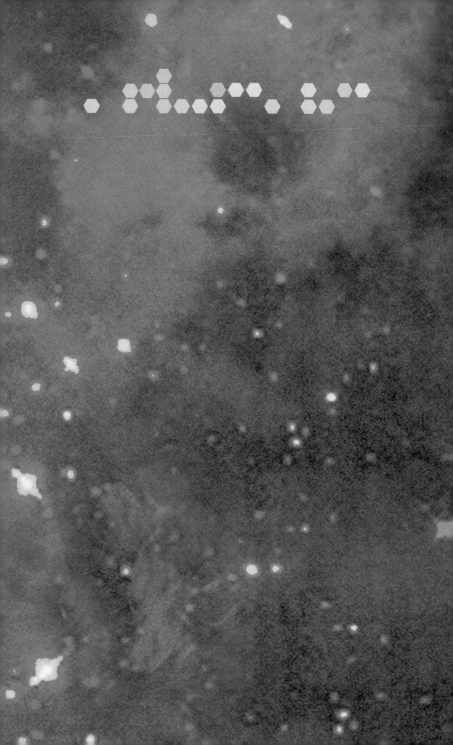

# CAPTAIN'S LOG

# THE *RAKK 'N' RUIN*

**Captain's Log! This is Rocket, captain of the starship *Rakk 'n' Ruin*!!!** Oh, man, it's great to be back on my old ship! And it's in pretty good shape. Since this restaurant never actually let any customers do anything but go straight to the bathroom, no children have ever actually played on the ship. No sticky fingerprints! No dirty-diaper surprises in the tunnel tubes!

sound of giant tree man throwing tunnel tubes, slides and other FunZone equipment out the door

The engines are in pretty good shape and it looks like the Groot Smoothies can be used as rocket fuel. I got a line hooked into the restaurant's power outlets to charge the weapons systems! Oh, how I love the sound of those words ... weapons systems! Weapons ... systems ... Plasma cannons ... Atomic disruptors ... Tachyon artillery ... Oh, I've missed you so much ...

sound of a single tear trickling down small woodland creature's face

# I AM GROOT...

Oh, yeah, we've run into one problem. The ship's computer was removed to make way for a diaper-changing area.

sound of giant tree man ripping diaper-changing area loose from wall and hurling it out window

The good news is we've got a lifetime supply of wet wipes ... The bad news is we have absolutely no way to steer or navigate.

(((•BING•))) TELL THEM ABOUT ME! TELL THEM ABOUT ME!

I'm getting to that. Will you chill out and let me do a proper Captain's Log for once? Okay, so we're gonna plug in Veronica and see if she can fly this thing.

((•BING•)) THIS IS NOT AN APPROVED USE, BUT ...

((•BING•)) HECK YEAH! LET'S DO IT! YEEEHAAAAAAW!!!!

**Okay, hold your horses!** We need to let the weapons systems ... ah ... charge up first. Then it's gonna go down like this:

1.  Blow the roof off this joint!

2.  Fly the *Rakk 'n' Ruin* through the hole in the roof and off this small, uncharted, extremely annoying planet.

3.  Attempt to blast our way through the swarm of space piranhas. We may die trying, but anything is better than staying in this shopping mall any longer.

4.  If we survive the space-piranha swarm ... locate a bathroom as soon as possible.

# I AM GROOT.

# THE PLAN

What do you mean you don't like the plan?

I AM GROOT.

What?

I AM GROOT.

Huh?

I AM GROOT.

You're kidding me, right?

I AM GROOT.

Okay, you're not kidding. But seriously, that's crazy.

I AM GROOT.

Oh, no, don't gimme that 'what it means to be a Guardian' thing again.

# I AM GROOT.

Aw, man ... I told you not to do that.

# I AM GROOT.

(((•BING•))) HE HAS A POINT, SMALL WOODLAND CREATURE.

You, too, Tape Dispenser?

(((•BING•))) I MAY NOT BE A GUARDIAN. I MAY ONLY BE A TOTALLY AWESOME TAPE DISPENSER. BUT WHEN I WAS CALLED UP TO SERVE THE GALAXY, I –

Okay, save it. Looks like we got a new plan:

1. This planet is not only small, uncharted and extremely annoying, it is also extremely dangerous!

2. There is a something under the surface. Something horrible ... something hungry ...

3. The shopping mall lures unsuspecting space shoppers to land on the planet and then the hungry something under the surface drags them down the toilet to their doom.

4. As Guardians of the Galaxy, Groot and I have a duty to destroy the evil, nasty, disgusting, horrible, hungry toilet monster so that the galaxy can once again be safe for people in search of bargain prices and chain-restaurant food!

Hey, Groot, just want to double-check. You SURE about this being our duty? Couldn't we just post a bad review of this place online?

# I AM GROOT.

Okay, gotcha ... It IS our duty ... so:

5. Groot and I are gonna go DOWN THE TOILET, find out what's down there and ...

6. I'm taking one of the ship's plasma cannons with me. I spliced on a trigger and a handle and I'm gonna blast a giant hole in whatever's down there.

7. Veronica has got the *Rakk 'n' Ruin* warmed up and ready to go in case it all goes wrong and we need to get the monkeybutt out of here in a furry hurry!

171

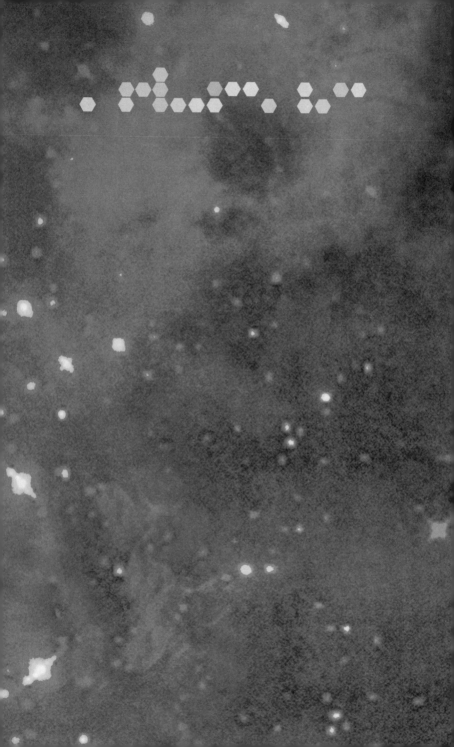

# CAPTAIN'S LOG

## 10

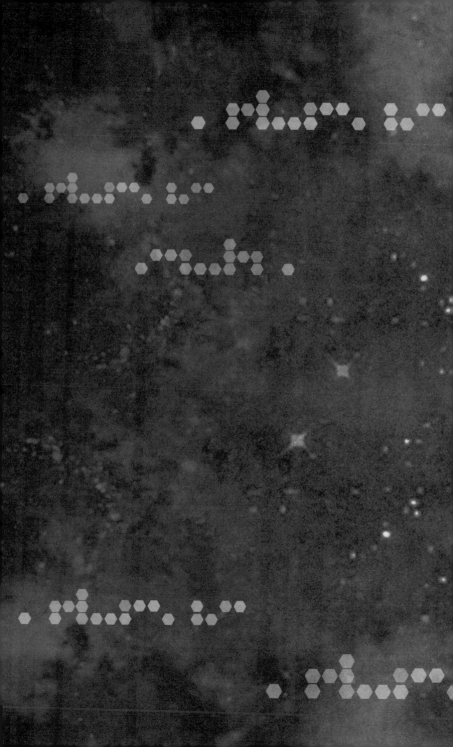

# DOWN THE TOILET

Captain's Log. This is Captain Rocket of the
*Rakk 'n' Ruin*.

Groot, Veronica and me are standing in front of
the bathroom door, ready to go down the drain to
whatever lies beneath the surface of this planet.
Before we go, possibly never to return, I thought
a quote from Shakespeare would be fitting:

'Once more unto the breach, dear friends, once
more.'

(((•BING•))) AS A SIMPLE TAPE DISPENSER, I CANNOT
UNDERSTAND POETRY. WHAT DOES THAT
MEAN?

No clue. Let's go.

sound of door opening

sound of carnivorous toilet gulping down
small woodland creature, giant tree man and
totally awesome tape dispenser

**AAAAAAAAAAAAAGHH!**

(((•BING•))) AAAAAAAAAAAAAAAGH!

# I AM GROOOOT.

sound of small woodland creature, giant tree
man and totally awesome tape dispenser
plunging for miles down dark tubes towards
incredibly smelly pale green light

sound of one big splash, one small
splash and one teeny-weeny totally
awesome splash

## Glrub! Blugggbbbh! Ptui! Sewage!!!!
## Deep sewage!!! I can't touch bottom!!!!

**No!!!!** I don't want to drown in an ocean of sewage! That's a really embarrassing thing to have written on your tombstone! Somebody save me ... Oh, wait, why aren't we sinking?

Oh, yeah, right, you can float. Whew! You don't mind if I just sort of ... ride on your head? Thanks,

pal, you're the best. You okay, Veronica? You're
waterproof, right?

(((•BING•))) YES, I'M JUST FINE.

Great. You know, I was sort of expecting like an
evil villain's hideout or something down here, but
sewage actually makes a lot of sense. We did just
come down a toilet hole.

# I AM GROOT.

Right, Groot. It's the amount of sewage that's a real surprise. I'd have to describe it as an ocean. An ocean of sewage that gives off its own pale green light and almost completely fills the inside of the planet.

# I AM GROOT.

Groot says it's nutritious and delicious ... Wait a minute, you're not actually drinking it, are you?

Well, I know you're thirsty – but seriously ... gross.

Oh, I see, you want to use it like fertilizer so you can grow really big and fight the huge monster that's in here with us. Wait, there's a huge monster in here with us? I don't see a huge monster.

sound of huge monster breaking the surface of the water and letting loose a terrifying roar

Drink up, Groot! This thing's huger than huge! I can't even think of a word huge enough to describe its **huge-osity**!

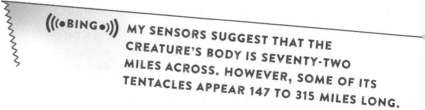

((( •BING•))) MY SENSORS SUGGEST THAT THE CREATURE'S BODY IS SEVENTY-TWO MILES ACROSS. HOWEVER, SOME OF ITS TENTACLES APPEAR 147 TO 315 MILES LONG.

Any idea what kind of creature it is? I'm guessing squid? Look at that giant eyeball glaring at us. Definitely a squid. Maybe an octopus?

I AM GROOT.

Okay, Groot thinks it's a Kraken. Is it a Kraken?

((( •BING•))) THAT'S A DIFFICULT QUESTION. I'LL NEED TO DOWNLOAD A DATABASE OF INSANELY LARGE SPACE PREDATORS.

Well, you better download quick ... because in about five seconds it's gonna be sushi. It's headed this way fast and as soon as the head is in range – kablooey!

sound of small woodland creature
unslinging plasma cannon from his back,
pointing it at unknown sewage monster and
chuckling gleefully

What do you mean which head? The giant monster
head right in front of us!

# I AM GROOT.

Behind me? Oh no, not two giant sewage monsters!

# I AM GROOT.

Oh no, not three giant sewage monsters!

Oh no, not eighteen giant sewage monsters!

((•BING•)) DID YOU JUST SAY EIGHTEEN?

YES! By the black hairs of my mask, there are eighteen giant sewage monsters, all with giant mouths filled with giant fangs and all headed this way fast!

((•BING•)) I HAVE JUST DOWNLOADED THE DATABASE OF INSANELY LARGE SPACE PREDATORS, AND YOUR DESCRIPTION HAS HELPED ME IDENTIFY THE MONSTER.

# You mean the **eighteen** monsters!!!!

**((•BING•))** NO, IT IS JUST ONE MONSTER. LISTEN TO THIS DESCRIPTION:

## THE COSMIC NAUTILUS

TYPE: SHELLFISH
HABITAT: DEEP SPACE
HEADS: EIGHTEEN

 TENTACLES: BETWEEN EIGHT AND FIFTY-THREE THOUSAND, PROBABLY CLOSER TO FIFTY-THREE THOUSAND.

SIZE: APPROXIMATELY THE SIZE OF A SMALL, UNCHARTED, ANNOYING PLANET.

 BEHAVIOUR: THE COSMIC NAUTILUS GROWS ELABORATE PATTERNS AND CONSTRUCTIONS ON ITS SHELL TO LURE PREY INTO LANDING ON ITS SURFACE.

DIET: EATS SPACE TOURISTS OF ALL SPECIES BUT PREFERS SMALL WOODLAND CREATURES.

Well, that answers a lot of questions, like why all that junk up top was made of shell. But it does leave one question unanswered.

(((•BING•))) WHAT IS THAT?

**WHICH HEAD AM I SUPPOSED TO SHOOT?????
THE PLASMA CANNON ONLY HAS ONE CHARGE!!!!
AND THE EIGHTEEN HEADS ARE ABOUT TEN
SECONDS FROM CHOMPING ON THE FINEST,
TASTIEST SMALL WOODLAND CREATURE THEY'VE
EVER SEEN!**

I AM GROOT.

What? What do you mean, you'll take care of it? Don't be crazy! That thing is about a thousand times bigger than you!

(((•BING•))) ONE THOUSAND AND EIGHTY-SEVEN TIMES BIGGER, TO BE EXACT.

sound of giant tree man guzzling the sewer
water and slurping it up through his roots!

Dude ... not only is that gross, it's NOT helping.

sound of REALLY giant tree
man growing

You're not really gonna try to make yourself one
thousand and eighty-seven times bigger, are you?

One thousand and eighty-eight? Well, that makes
sense in a COMPLETELY CRAZY sort of way!

sound of REALLY, REALLY giant tree man
slurping and growing

Dude, you have sucked up about half the water in here! I think it's making the heads mad! Not that it really matters, since they were already planning to eat us ...

sound of REALLY, REALLY, REALLY
giant tree man wrestling with cosmic
nautilus heads

# I AMMM GROOT.

**Dude ... ouch!** Now that you're like eighty miles tall, you're gonna need to use your indoor voice.

sound of REALLY, REALLY, REALLY, REALLY, REALLY giant tree man growing countless smaller branches and countless smaller branches on those branches and countless smaller branches on those branches until most of the heads can barely move

# I AMMM GROOT.

Uh, remember what I said about the indoor voice ... Whisper, dude ...

# I AM GROOOOT.

So you're saying you've got seventeen of the heads in headlocks but you can't get the last one? No problem! I was feeling kind of left out, anyway.

**OKAY! HEAD EIGHTEEN! HERE I AM!!!! I TASTE GREAT!!!!** C'MON OVER FOR A NIBBLE ... and a blast in the face from a plasma cannon.

sound of one cosmic nautilus head slithering its way towards small woodland creature and slightly worried tape dispenser

sound of small woodland creature aiming plasma cannon and chuckling gleefully

What do you mean, don't shoot it? That's what I do!
I shoot things!

I thought you were the one who wanted to rid the
universe of this evil freak?

Not evil?

I AM GROOT.

Just hungry?

I AM GROOT.

Okay, fine, then let me ask you one question: if I don't blast it, then what am I supposed to do, let it eat me and leave you here to play Twister with it forever?

The SHELL? What good is it going to do to shoot the shell?

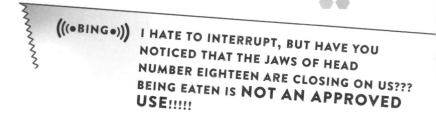

(((•BING•))) I HATE TO INTERRUPT, BUT HAVE YOU NOTICED THAT THE JAWS OF HEAD NUMBER EIGHTEEN ARE CLOSING ON US??? BEING EATEN IS **NOT AN APPROVED** USE!!!!!

You're sure about this, Groot? You want me to shoot the shell – not the giant head that's **ABOUT TO EAT ME**?

Okay, pal. Hang on!

sound of plasma cannon erupting

sound of plasma torpedo hitting inside
of shell

sound of shell cracking open, creating a hole
several miles wide

sound of giant tree man hurling cosmic
nautilus through the hole in its own
shell into deep space

Listen, pal, I'll be glad to tell you how awesome
that was later ... but right now, I need you to get
us back to the surface fast. I think the toilets are
gonna be safe to use now and it's an emergency.

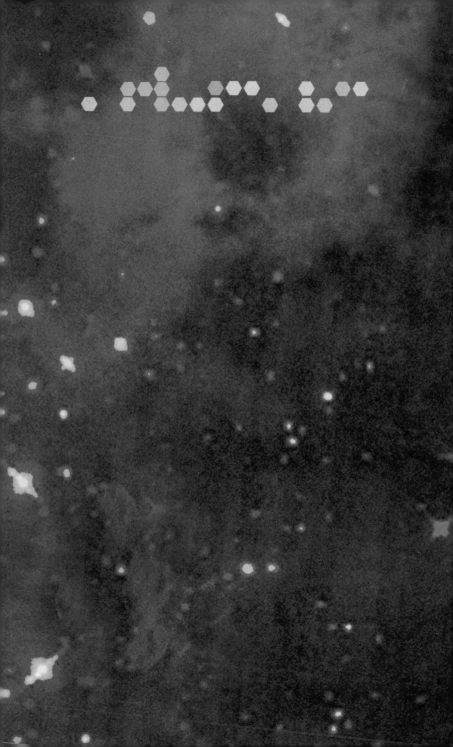

# CAPTAIN'S LOG
# 11

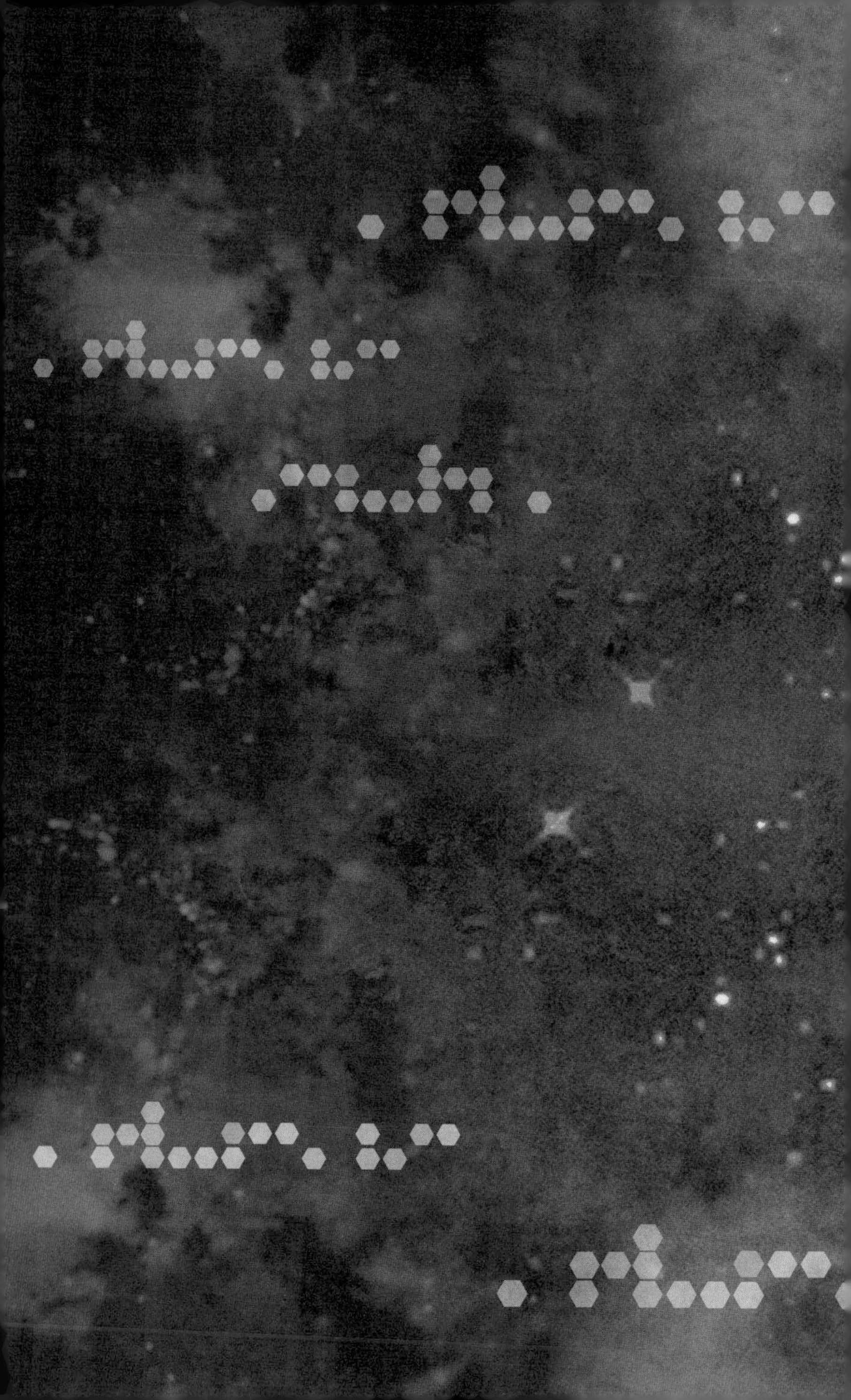

# SQUID SURPRISE

Captain's Log. This is –

 I CAN'T FIND CAPTAIN SLOG IN YOUR CONTACT LIST. WOULD YOU LIKE ME TO –

## LOG!!! LOG!!!! IT'S TWO WORDS!!!!!

 HEE-HEE.

You mean you've been pulling my tail with that Captain Slog thing?

# Don't encourage her, Groot!!!

This is important. It's hopefully our final log entry for this small, uncharted, incredibly annoying planet.

Okay ... Captain's Log. This is Captain Rocket of the *Rakk 'n' Ruin*. Me, Groot and Veronica are standing in the rubble of a planet-sized shopping mall. The plasma cannon created a massive earthquake that knocked down just about every chain store in sight. Luckily, one Yak-Fil-A was still standing so I did get to use the bathroom.

All the killer robots stopped working when Groot threw out the nautilus. Apparently, it was controlling them telepathically and powering them with the fuel from the spaceships it captured.

Anyway, Groot has spent the last couple hours downsizing and now he's small enough to fit in the *Rakk 'n' Ruin*. He passed the time by doodling on the touchscreen. Hey, let me see what you drew ...

**... Dude, that ain't bad. You could sell that, like on a T-shirt or something.**

I AM GROOT.

You're welcome. Okay, meanwhile, Veronica has been warming up the ship and I've reattached the plasma cannon, so we should be ready to go soon.

I AM GROOT.

Right. Groot just pointed out that the planet is still surrounded by a swarm of giant space piranhas.

But we can't stay here, because there's no food, water or soil. Also, it's really annoying.

Everybody prepare for an epic space-piranha battle that's even more epic than the LAST epic space-piranha battle.

# ONCE MORE UNTO THE BREACH!

awkward silence

Blast off!

awkward silence

Veronica?

(((•BING•))) YES, SMALL WOODLAND CREATURE? HOW MUCH TAPE DO YOU NEED?

NO! I don't need any tape! You're the ship's computer now, remember? When I say blast off, you blast off!

((•BING•)) OH, YES. I FORGOT.

awkward silence

Why aren't you blasting off?

((•BING•)) OH, SORRY, I THOUGHT YOU WERE GONNA SAY THAT SHAKESPEARE THING AGAIN.

Would you just blast off alr—

sound of *Rakk 'n' Ruin* rising majestically in the air, turning slowly towards the heavens and then blasting off under the skilful control of a totally awesome tape dispenser

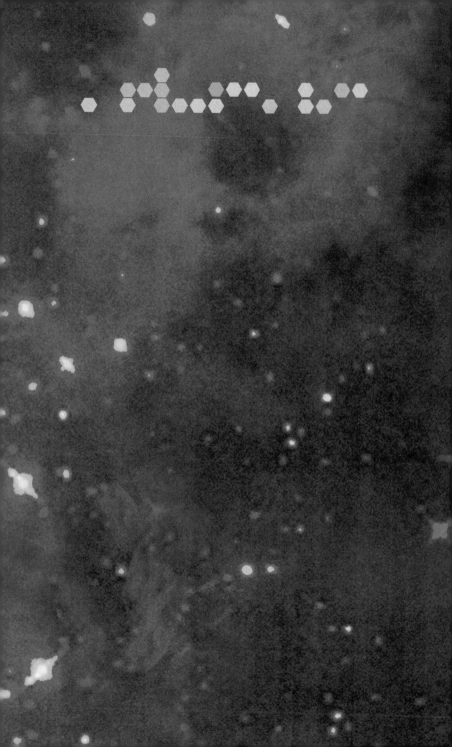

# CAPTAIN'S LOG
# 12

# BLAST OFF

Captain's Log. This is Captain Rocket of the *Rakk 'n' Ruin*. We've lifted off from the planet and are coming up on the swarm of space piranhas FAST!

Okay, guys, get ready to fire all of our guns at once and ex— **WHAT THE HAMSTER HEINIE IS THAT????**

((•BING•)) IT APPEARS TO BE A COSMIC NAUTILUS LOCKED IN A DEATHLY STRUGGLE WITH A SWARM OF SPACE PIRANHAS.

They're totally ignoring us! But the squid isn't!

((•BING•)) IT'S A NAUTILUS.

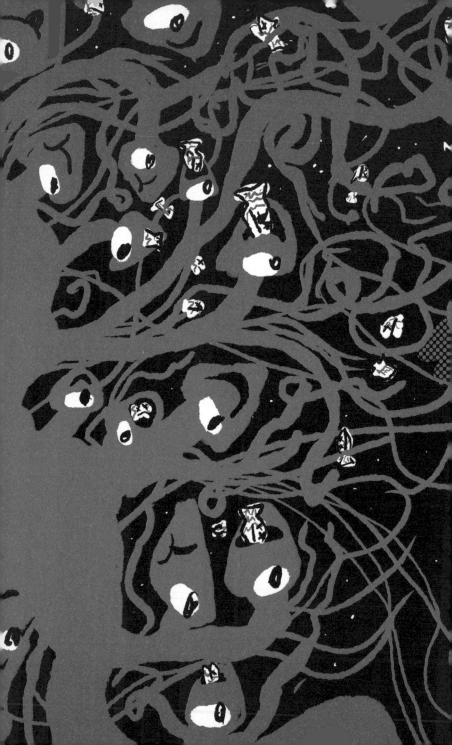

Yeah, yeah, it's wriggling a couple thousand
tentacles in our direction! Prepare to open fire ...

# I AM GROOT.

What? Oh, yeah, you're right. It's just waving.
It looks kind of ... happy. It's having its best day
ever stuffing space piranhas in its eighteen
mouths! Okay, have fun, squid dude!

sound of small woodland creature, giant tree
man and totally awesome tape dispenser
waving to cosmic nautilus

## And now let's get the
monkeybutt out of here!

sound of *Rakk 'n' Ruin* hyperspeeding
through space on its way to Rocket and
Groot and Veronica's next adventure!

# AND SO WE SAY FAREWELL TO OUR HEROES AS THEY ZOOM TRIUMPHANTLY ACROSS THE GALAXY!*

*Until they run out of Groot Smoothie rocket fuel, which is going to be a lot sooner than they think!

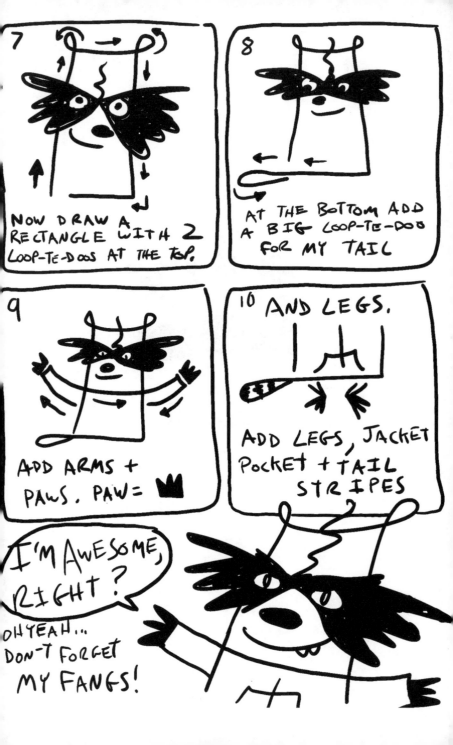

# THE END

for now ...